To my editor, Liz Bicknell
N. W.

To all the homeschooled backyard inventors out there
K. H.

First edition 2015

Library of Congress Catalog Card Number 2014944794
ISBN 978-0-7636-5476-4

14 15 16 17 18 19 CCP 10 9 8 7 6 5 4 3 2 1

Printed in Shenzhen, Guangdong, China

This book was typeset in Garamond.
The illustrations were done in pen and ink with pastel.

Candlewick Press
99 Dover Street
Somerville, Massachusetts 02144

visit us at www.candlewick.com

THE THREE MOUTHS OF LITTLE TOM DRUM

NANCY WILLARD

ILLUSTRATED BY

KEVIN HAWKES

CANDLEWICK PRESS

ꞨNCE THERE WAS A BOY called Little Tom Drum who could never get his fill of strawberry pie. You may have seen him with his mother in the supermarket, lingering in the fresh-fruit aisle or pausing before the shelves of frozen peas and strawberries.

The night before his eighth birthday party, his mother baked a strawberry pie and left it on the windowsill in the kitchen to cool by the light of the full moon.

"Mom, can I have one slice of pie before I go to bed?"

His mother shook her head. "What if our guests want seconds? There won't be enough to go around."

"Just one slice?" pleaded Little Tom Drum.

"Just one slice, then," said his mother.

And she cut a very thin slice and put it on a china plate, and Little Tom Drum took the butter knife and cut it into six pieces to make it seem like more, and he ate them slowly, slowly, slowly, but he could never get his fill of strawberry pie.

"Mom, can I have just one more slice?"

"I think not," said his mother.

"A very thin slice?"

"Have you three mouths?" said his mother, laughing.

"Oh, I wish I did," said Little Tom Drum.

His mother set the pie and the knife on the windowsill, where the moon admired them.

Little Tom Drum went to bed but not to sleep. In the room next to his, he heard his father's shoes drop — *bing, bang!* He heard his mother locking the front door. Then he heard nothing. Everyone was asleep except Little Tom Drum.

"How lonely it must be in the kitchen," said Little Tom Drum.

He climbed out of bed.

"The pie must be very sad. I shall visit the pie."

He climbed up on a chair.
"Hello, pie."

In its silver pan, it looked as large and as golden as the harvest moon and certainly more than enough for ten. Little Tom Drum took the knife and cut himself a piece, and he chewed it slowly, slowly, slowly. Suddenly he heard footsteps. But when he tried to climb down, the chair tipped over. Light streamed into the kitchen.

"Aha!" said his mother. "Stealing the pie!"

"Oh, Mom, I can never get enough strawberry pie," cried the three mouths of Little Tom Drum.

"Mercy!" shrieked his mother. "There's a monster in the house!"

Then Little Tom Drum caught sight of his reflection in the shiny pan, and what did he see? A new mouth on his left cheek and a new mouth on his right cheek and his old mouth in the middle.

His father came running.

"Mom and Dad, it's only me," called the three mouths in unison.

When they saw it really was their son, they burst into tears, and the three mouths of Little Tom Drum cried loudest of all.

At last his mother wiped her eyes on her sleeve and said, "We must cancel the party. I'll call the guests first thing in the morning."

"I can't have my party?" cried the three mouths of Little Tom Drum.

"How can we? What would people say?" said his mother.

As soon as the moon slipped away and the sun woke up, his mother carried the pie outside and threw it into the darkest, farthest corner of the garden where not even weeds would grow.

"Naturally you can't go to school," said his father. "We must hire a tutor to come and teach you at home."

"I can't go to school?" cried the three mouths of Little Tom Drum.

"How can you go to school? What would people say?" said his father.

So Little Tom Drum did not go to school.

His mother gave him a toy octopus with movable arms and a tabby kitten to keep him company. And very good company Tabby was, except for her habit of jumping on his head every morning when she wanted to be fed.

The tutor came every day and brought him books. Little Tom Drum read and read and read. He read books on mathematics and giraffes and gardening.

When he read aloud at the dinner table from a book on elephants, his mother let him play with her elephant salt and pepper shakers.

And when he finished reading a very long book on the invention of the bicycle, his father gave him a bicycle that was just the right size for him.

During recess, the tutor played ball with him.

"A brilliant pupil," said the tutor. "Someday he'll be a great inventor."

His father built him a workshop full of tables and tools in the backyard, big enough to hold his inventions.

His first invention was a telescope with ears. He said to its left ear, "Show me the playground at school." And the telescope showed him the playground, but it was very far away.

Then he mounted the telescope on the roof and said to its right ear, "Show me what my friends are doing."

The telescope let him look right into the school yard and see his old friends playing on the swings, the seesaw, and the jungle gym. This pleased the parents of Little Tom Drum, but every night his mother whispered to his father, "It's all very well to have an inventor in the family, but what will happen to him when he grows up?"

And though nobody spoke of it, they all wished he would find the face he'd lost, and nobody wished it more than Little Tom Drum.

On his ninth birthday, with one breath he blew out all the candles on his birthday cake.

The next morning he found on the doorstep of his workshop a plain white box. On the box was written:

Wishing Machine
What is your wish? Speak clearly, please.

He tore open the box. One half of the box contained a pie pan, a knife, a bicycle wheel, two small elephants, one stargazer lily, a baseball, and a baby octopus. The other half contained a large sheet on which was printed a lovely drawing that showed, in ten steps, how to assemble the wishing machine. A stranger machine was never seen.

"Please take away these three mouths and give me back the face I lost," said Little Tom Drum to the box.

Nothing happened. He was about to repeat his wish when he spied the fine print under the stargazer lily.

Please assemble the machine.

Little Tom Drum set to work putting the pieces together. He twisted the arms of the octopus around the spokes of the bicycle wheel, just as the picture showed him.

He put the elephants on the rim of the wheel and the baseball in the middle. He followed the directions very carefully, and when he added the last piece, which was the stargazer lily, he held his breath.

Your wish has been received. Please wait.

And while he was waiting, he invented an electric skateboard, a hat tipper, and a cat petter for a woman with fifteen cats.

Many people wrote to him about their problems.

My dog lost his left paw in an accident. Can you make him another one?

Little Tom Drum made the dog another one. It was invisible, but you could see the tracks it left in the dirt.

My grandma walks real slow. Can you make her some speedy shoes?

Little Tom Drum made her some speedy shoes. They were made with wings that he designed himself, and those shoes flew so fast, they could take her to tomorrow and back before sunrise.

And when people discovered that he could play three harmonicas at once and blow a hundred soap bubbles from three bubble pipes, they stopped by just to watch him.

"In a person so brilliant, what does it matter how many mouths he has?" said his fans.

He could sing three different songs at once and make them harmonize.

One day three children on their way to school took a shortcut through his backyard.

And what did they see there but an old bicycle wheel with an octopus and two small elephants attached to it, half buried in dirt and ferns?

They ran to Little Tom Drum, who was busy blowing one hundred bubbles for his mother and father.

"Little Tom Drum!" they cried. "We found a funny machine in your backyard!"

Little Tom Drum followed them, and when he saw the machine, he said, "That is a wishing machine."

"How does it work? How does it work?" clamored the children.

"I don't know. I got the pieces for making it but not the directions for using it. I made it when I wished I could look like everybody else."

The machine whirred ever so softly, as if it were waking from a long sleep.

"We don't want you to look like everybody else!" shouted the oldest child. "We just wish you could be Little Tom Drum forever and ever."

The machine whirred again and rose into the air like a soap bubble and vanished.

And lo and behold, there stood Little Tom Drum in his nightshirt, his face covered with strawberry pie, just as he'd stood in his mother's kitchen the night before his eighth birthday.

When his mother and father saw him, they nearly fell off the porch.

"Mercy!" shrieked his mother. "It's our own Little Tom Drum!"

His mother and father cried and laughed, and the children laughed loudest of all. At last his mother wiped her eyes on her sleeve.

"Shall we have the party?"

Of course the children who found the machine were invited. So was the woman with fifteen cats and the dog who had lost a paw and the grandmother whose speedy shoes never wore out, along with five other grandmothers who had ordered the same shoes for themselves. Little Tom Drum's mother baked three strawberry pies: a small one for the grown-ups, who were afraid of gaining weight; a big one for the children, who were afraid of not getting seconds; and the biggest one of all for Little Tom Drum. He ate it right down to the last crumb.

"How about one more slice?" said his mother.

"I think not," said Little Tom Drum.